The Great White Man-Eating Shark

There are lots of Early Reader
stories you might enjoy.

Look at the back of the book or,
for a complete list, visit
www.orionbooks.co.uk

The Great White Man-Eating Shark

Margaret Mahy

Illustrated by
Jonathan Allen

Orion
Children's Books

The *Great White Man Eating Shark*
was originally published in 1989
by J.M. Dent & Sons
This edition first published in Great Britain in 2015
by Orion Children's Books
an imprint of Hachette Children's Group
and published by Hodder & Stoughton

Orion House
5 Upper Saint Martin's Lane
London WC2H 9EA
An Hachette UK Company

1 3 5 7 9 10 8 6 4 2

Text © Margaret Mahy 1989
Illustrations © Jonathan Allen 1989

The right of Margaret Mahy and Jonathan Allen to be identified
as author and illustrator of this work has been asserted.

The paper and board used in this paperback are natural and
recyclable products made from wood grown in sustainable forests.
The manufacturing processes conform to the environmental
regulations of the country of origin.

A catalogue record for this book is available from the British Library.

ISBN 978 1 4440 1438 9

Printed and bound in China

www.orionchildrensbooks.co.uk

There was once a boy called
Norvin who was a good actor but
rather plain.

In fact, he looked very like
a shark. He had small sharkish
eyes, a pointed sharkish head and
sharp sharkish teeth.

Unfortunately, there are not many plays written with good parts for sharks so Norvin took up swimming instead.

He soon became a good swimmer and learned to shoot through the water like a silver arrow.

14

Norvin lived near a wonderful bathing beach called Caramel Cove, but he had to share it with lots of other swimmers.

When Norvin tried shooting
through the water like a silver
arrow the other swimmers got in
his way.

This made him cross and
resentful.

"What's the use of being able to shoot through the water like a silver arrow if everyone gets in my way?" he thought.

So he came up with a wicked plan.

Out of plastic he made himself
the dorsal fin of a great white
man-eating shark.

Then he strolled around the headland, thought a few sharkish thoughts, strapped it on and slid into the clear blue water.

Mrs Scorpio, who ran the
cake-shop, was bobbing harmlessly
up and down in the waves when
suddenly she saw the dorsal fin of
a great white man-eating shark
heading straight for her.

If you are swimming and see
a great white man-eating shark
heading straight for you, the
thing to do is leave the water in a
quiet and dignified way. But Mrs
Scorpio did not know this.

"Shark! Shark!" she yelled
and flung herself on to the sand,
screaming and kicking
with terror.

What a panic there was! Up
and down Caramel Cove people
grabbed up their children, their
dogs and inflatable canoes.

Within moments the sand was crowded with dripping bodies and the sea was completely empty. Everyone stared despairingly at the cruising dorsal fin.

Many people thought they could just make out the shape of a great white man-eating shark cutting through the water beneath it.

Norvin wore the expression
a great white man-eating shark
always wears when it is hungry,
and his acting was so good that,
even when he came up to breathe,
people were convinced he was
actually looking for prey.

It was a very hot day, but
nobody dared go swimming again.

Norvin had the whole of
Caramel Cove to himself. He spent
all afternoon shooting backwards
and forwards like a silver arrow.

Everyone else watched enviously, sighing and rubbing suntan cream on to one another. No one dared to share the sea with a great white man-eating shark.

At last, Norvin swam out around the headland and vanished from sight. After that, everyone except Norvin was too scared to go swimming at Caramel Cove.

"Norvin! Come out at once,"
his friends all cried.

"There is a great white
man-eating shark hanging
around these parts."

Norvin laughed.

"Nonsense!" he said. "It is probably only a whale shark, or even a basking shark . . .

They are vegetarians, you know."
Norvin had the entire beach to
himself for three whole days.

However, soon a few brave people, tired of seeing Norvin shooting to and fro like a silver arrow, started swimming again.

Others joined them, and soon
everyone was splashing around
happily once more, enjoying the
swimming and the summer.

But Norvin had grown used to
having the beach to himself.

He strolled around the
headland, put on his dorsal fin,
and swam back into Caramel Cove.

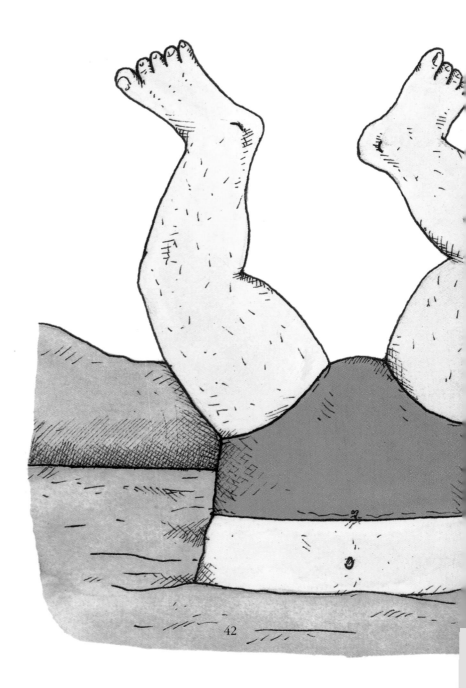

Mr Dorsey, the plumber, was showing his little boy, Courtney, how to stand on his head in the water – something a plumber sometimes has to do.

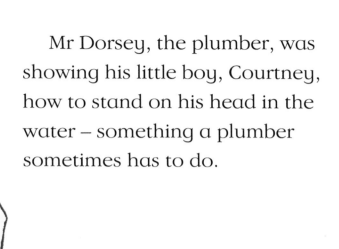

Suddenly, he found himself
nose to nose with Norvin. He did
not recognise Norvin, of course. He
thought he was nose to nose with
a great white man-eating shark.

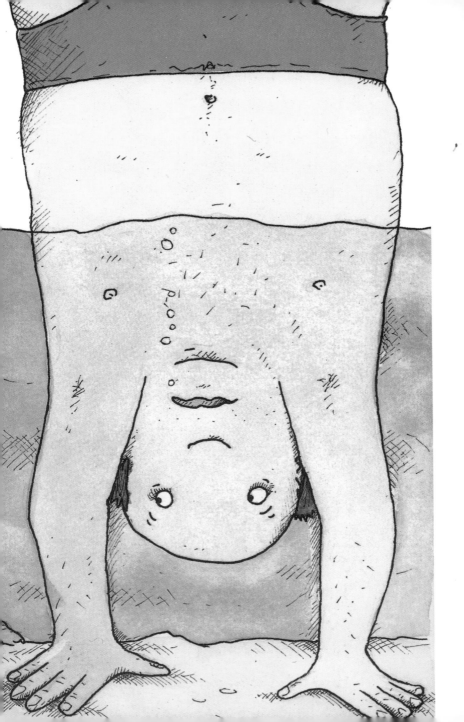

If you find yourself nose to nose with a shark, the thing to do is to leave the water quietly – just as if your only thought was to rub in more suntan lotion. Mr Dorsey did not know this.

"Shark! Shark!" he yelled. Grabbing up Courtney, he flung himself on to the sand, kicking and screaming in terror.

Within minutes Norvin had the
beach all to himself once more.
No one dared go swimming for a
week at Caramel Cove . . .

No one except Norvin, that is.
He shot to and fro like a silver
arrow, while others watched
longingly from the beach.

Soon they could stand it
no longer. A few brave people
decided to take a risk.

Caramel Cove was once more
splashing and bubbling with
happy swimmers.

Norvin, however, was becoming greedy. He wanted Caramel Cove all to himself, all the time. So he strolled around the headland and put on his dorsal fin once more.

Then he swam back to Caramel Cove, laughing to himself as he thought of all the terror he would cause.

But, suddenly, he felt he was
not alone. Someone was swimming
beside him. Who could it be? He
looked out of the corner of his eye.

There, nuzzling up to him, was
a great white man-eating shark –
a female.

Norvin was such a good actor that she did not realise he was merely pretending to be a shark. She gave him a very loving glance.

"You are the shark of my dreams," she said. "Marry me at once or I shall lose my temper and bite you!"

He shot like a silver arrow, dorsal fin and all, towards the beach and flung himself on to the sand where he lay, kicking and screaming with terror.

Everyone could see at a glance what Norvin had been up to.

The people of Caramel Cove
put up a shark net across the
mouth of the bay,

but for the rest of the summer
Norvin sat on the beach, watching
other swimmers shoot backwards
and forwards like silver arrows.

He had had such a terrible
shock that – shark net or not – he
was too frightened to go swimming
for a long, long time. Though he
was a plain boy, he had made
rather a good-looking shark, and I
think he was very wise not to take
any dangerous chances.

What are you going to read next?

Have more adventures with Horrid Henry,

or save the day with Anthony Ant!

Become a superhero with Monstar,

float off to sea with Algy,

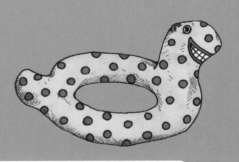